This edition published by
Coles, Canada
by arrangement with Twin Books

© 1992 Twin Books UK Ltd

Produced by
TWIN BOOKS
Kimbolton House
117A Fulham Road
London SW3 6RL
England

Directed by CND – Muriel Nathan-Deiller
Illustrated by Van Gool-Lefèvre-Loiseaux
Text adapted by Barbara Paulding Thrasher

ISBN: 1-85469-959-8

Printed in Hong Kong

"'VAN GOOL'S'"

Little Red Riding Hood

TWIN BOOKS

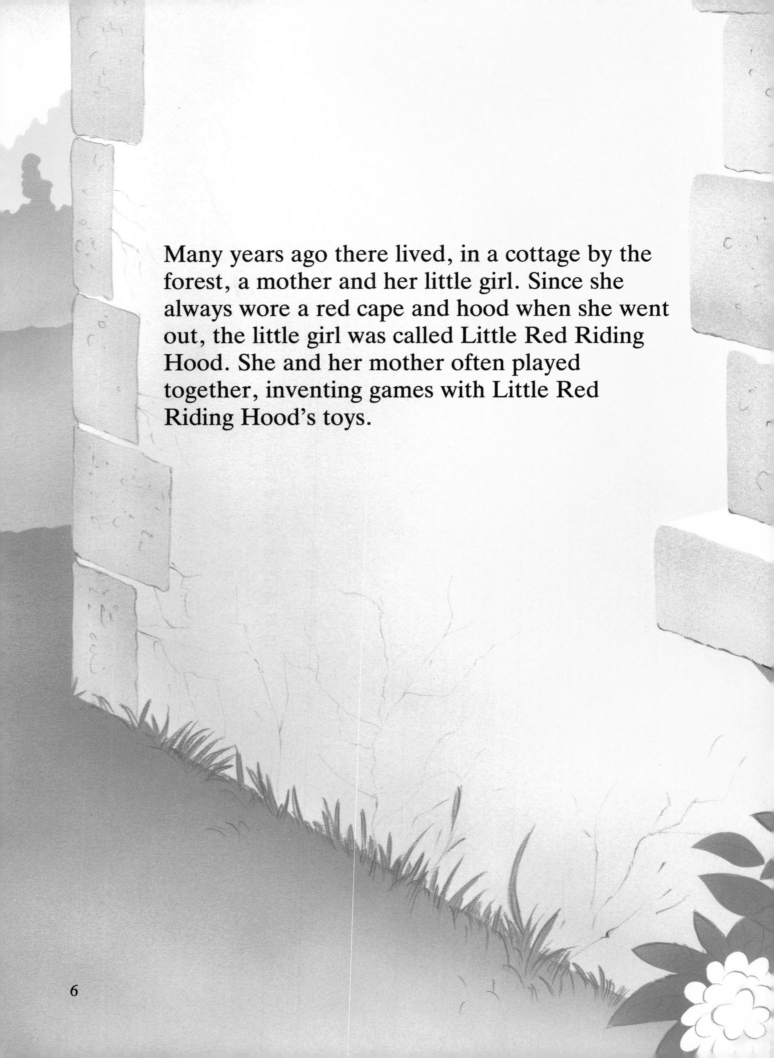

Many years ago there lived, in a cottage by the forest, a mother and her little girl. Since she always wore a red cape and hood when she went out, the little girl was called Little Red Riding Hood. She and her mother often played together, inventing games with Little Red Riding Hood's toys.

6

One day in springtime, Little Red Riding Hood's grandmother became ill, and so the mother made her a pie. Little Red Riding Hood's mother hummed as she rolled the dough and cut the apples, and soon the pie was ready.

Together they packed the pie, and a jar of jelly that the girl had made herself, into a basket for Grandmother, who lived in a cottage at the far side of the forest.

"Take this to Grandmother. It will make her feel better," said Little Red Riding Hood's mother, fastening her cape. "And she will be happy to see you. Keep to the path, my dear, so you won't get lost. And don't talk to strangers. Tell Grandmother I'll visit her tomorrow."

"Okay, Mother," replied the girl. "And I'll hurry right home before dinner."

Little Red Riding Hood was pleased to be entrusted with such an important task. She waved to her mother as she set off on her way. The sun shone brightly, and it seemed that even the flowers waved as they moved in the warm spring breeze. As she walked deeper into the forest, the trees' branches overhead blocked out much of the sunlight. "The path is like a delightful cave!" thought the girl, and she began to skip.

Because Little Red Riding Hood was so kind and gentle, the forest animals liked her. Before long the girl noticed that her animal friends were coming with her. The birds flitted from tree to bush, and the squirrels raced along the branches. Perhaps they thought she was too little to make such a long journey alone.

"It's a lovely day for a walk through the forest," said Little Red Riding Hood, and the animals with her agreed.

The friendly girl was so happy that she didn't notice a wolf approaching. The frightened forest creatures began to scurry away.

"What is that sound?" Little Red Riding Hood asked herself. She could hear heavy footsteps. Suddenly, from behind the trees the wolf appeared.

18

"Goodness! You startled me," said Little Red Riding Hood. She didn't know enough about wolves to be frightened of this one.

"Did I?" replied the wolf, thinking what a tasty treat the girl would make. "Well, I'm just out having my morning stroll."

Without warning the wolf dashed away. Little Red Riding Hood turned to see lumberjacks walking through the forest. They passed nearby, whistling and chatting as they went.

When the forest was quiet again, the wolf stepped out from behind a tree. Little Red Riding Hood had forgotten her mother's warning not to speak to strangers. "I'm on my way to my grandmother's cottage at the other side of the forest," she said. The wolf nodded, wondering how he could delay her and get to the cottage first. Then he could have both her and her grandmother for lunch!

Suddenly, the crafty wolf had an idea. "I think a bouquet of wildflowers would cheer the old lady," he said brightly.

"What a grand idea!" replied Little Red Riding Hood. "I'll pick her some flowers right away. How happy she'll be!"

"I'll be on my way now," said the wolf. "I'm sure we'll meet again."

"I hope so!" said the girl.

The wolf sauntered into the woods, but as soon as he was out of sight . . .

. . . he raced away, running as fast as he could toward Grandmother's cottage. "This is my lucky day," he thought. "Not one, but *two* meals for my hungry tummy." He knew just where the cottage was, so he wasted no time heading toward it, leaping over logs and dodging trees.

Little Red Riding Hood ran to find her forest friends. "Guess what?" she asked them. "I met the nicest fellow, and he suggested I take Granny a bouquet. Isn't that a fine idea?"

"I know where the prettiest flowers are!" exclaimed one of the squirrels, pointing into the forest.

Little Red Riding Hood and the animals wandered in the woods until they came to a clearing. She had also forgotten her mother's warning not to stray off the path!

Beautiful wildflowers grew all about the sunny clearing. Little Red Riding Hood stooped to pick them, and in no time had gathered an armful. "What pretty flowers," she said. "I'll have to thank Mr. Wolf for his advice."

The squirrels looked at each other. "Mr. Wolf?" squeaked one of them with alarm. They scurried after the girl.

32

In the meantime, the wolf had arrived, panting from his long run, at Grandmother's cottage. He leaped over the picket fence, then he sat down to catch his breath.

Inside the cottage Grandmother was sleeping peacefully. The wolf outside tried to remember what Little Red Riding Hood's voice sounded like, then he trotted to the door.

33

The wolf knocked at the door rather heavily.

"Who is it?" came Grandmother's voice.

"It's Little Red Riding Hood," answered the wolf, mimicking the girl's voice as best he could.

"The door's unlocked. Come in, my dear," replied Grandmother.

The hungry wolf opened the door and glanced about the room. Then he bounded toward Grandmother's bed, and before she knew what was happening . . .

. . . he had gobbled her up in one mouthful. The squirrels and mice arrived on the windowsill just in time to see the wolf's crime. They looked at each other with alarm. "Little Red Riding Hood will be next on his menu!" exclaimed the squirrel.

"We must get help!" squeaked the mice. The animals raced off into the forest.

The wolf waddled about the cottage. He found one of Grandmother's nightgowns and nightcaps, and slipped these on. He pulled the cap over his big ears, then got into bed and pulled the covers up around his chin.

The wolf was almost asleep, for he was feeling full, when he heard a knock at the door. Doing his best to imitate Grandmother's voice, he called out, "Who is it?"

"It's Little Red Riding Hood," came the reply.

"Come right in, dear," replied the wolf.

Little Red Riding Hood unlatched the door and stepped into the cottage. "My, it's dark in here, Granny," she said. She tried to sound cheery, but she felt very uneasy.

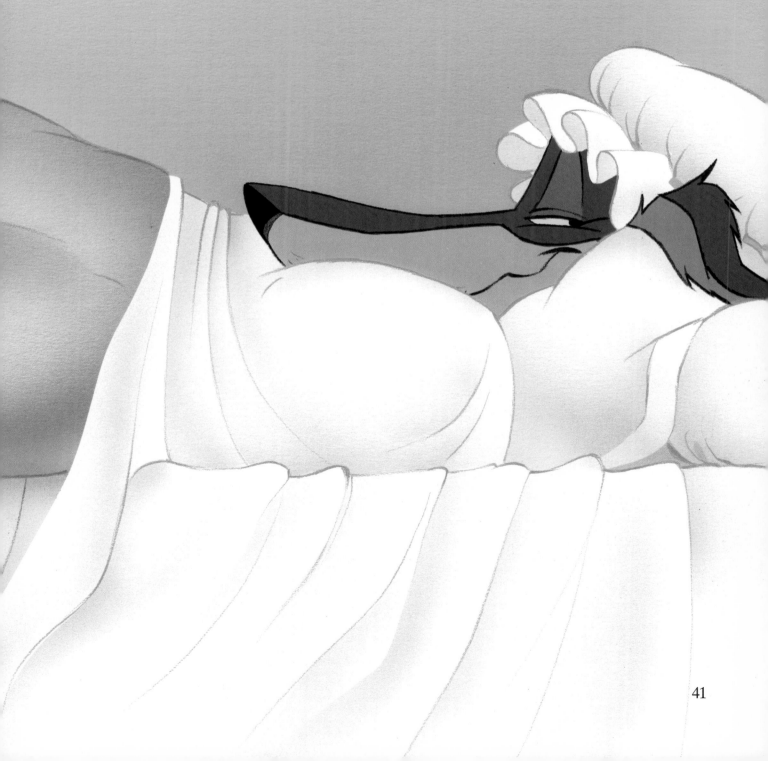

Just then the mice had found a family of Little Red Riding Hood's rabbit friends in the forest. "Come quick!" exclaimed the mouse. "The wolf has eaten Little Red Riding Hood's grandmother, and he will eat her next! Hurry! We must save her!"

The forest animals ran as fast as they could toward Grandmother's cottage.

At the cottage, Little Red Riding Hood
was unpacking the basket.

"I've brought you some food from mother,"
she said, setting the gifts on the table, "and
some flowers to make you feel better."

She glanced at the wolf. "My goodness,
Grandmother, you don't look at all like
yourself," said the girl. "You must be very
sick."

45

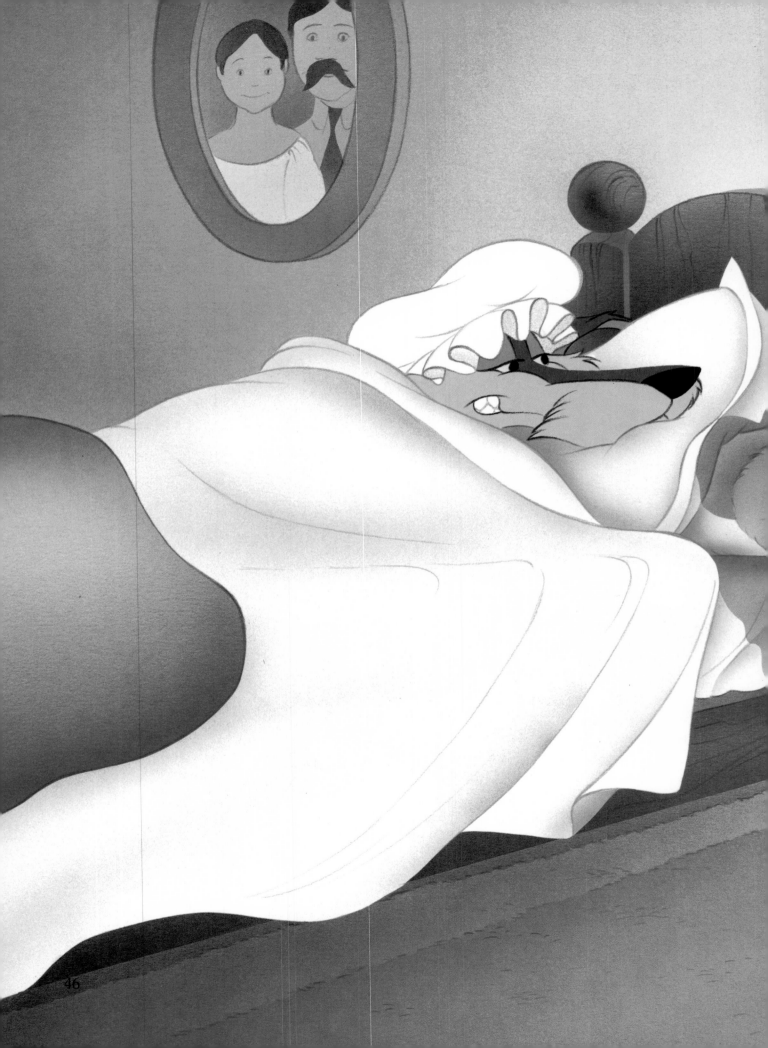

Little Red Riding Hood sat down next to Grandmother's bed. "My, Grandmother," she said with alarm, "what big eyes you have!"

"All the better to see you with, my dear," croaked the wolf. Just then his ears popped out from under the nightcap.

"Ah, Grandmother. But what big ears you have," said the girl.

"All the better to hear you with," replied the wolf.

"Grandmother! What big teeth you have!" said Little Red Riding Hood.

"All the better to eat you with!" cried the wolf, leaping out of the bed.

The wolf swallowed her in one gulp.

He took off Grandmother's clothes. Then he sniffed at the pie, but he was too full to eat another bite.

50

Feeling very heavy indeed, he walked slowly out of the cottage into the barn. He was looking for a place to take a long nap, and the hay looked inviting.

The wolf was so sleepy that he took no notice of the mice and squirrels, chattering in the barn loft. If he had listened to what they were saying, he would have taken note of them, for they were busy planning his downfall.

"The pitchfork is ready!" called one of the squirrels.

"The rope is ready!" called another.

"Patience!" said one of the mice. "Wait until he's in just the right spot."

The animals held their breath as the wolf ambled into range, and then . . .

. . . *Bonk*! The squirrels let go of the pitchfork handle, and it landed squarely on the wolf's head.

"Bull's-eye!" shouted one of the squirrels. The wolf lay on the ground in a daze.

Quickly, a mouse tied the rope to the wolf's tail. Throwing the rope over a rafter and threading it through a pulley, the animals began hoisting the wolf into the air.

When the wolf was fully suspended in the air by his tail, Grandmother and Little Red Riding Hood tumbled out of his open mouth, and landed on the soft hay.

The animals cheered when they saw the two were unharmed, and a bunny explained how they had performed the rescue. Little Red Riding Hood was terribly shaken, but grateful to her animal friends.

"I shall never trust a wolf again," exclaimed the girl. "And when Mother tells me to keep to the path, and not speak to strangers, I will do just that!"

Grandmother invited everyone to have some pie. The wolf, in the meantime, had dragged himself up and was slinking into the forest.

"Shoo, now! Shoo!" shouted Grandmother after him.

The wolf was soon hungry again. Wherever he wandered from that time on, the forest animals remembered his naughty exploit. "Foolish wolf! Foolish wolf!" the birds would call. And as for Little Red Riding Hood, she listened more carefully to her mother, and every morning she scattered bread crumbs and seeds for the animals who had rescued her.